Firetrucks

by Peter Brady

Bridgestone Books
an Imprint of Capstone Press

Bridgestone Books are published by Capstone Press
818 North Willow Street, Mankato, Minnesota 56001
Copyright © 1996 by Capstone Press
Printed in the United States of America

Library of Congress Cataloging-in-Publication Data
Brady, Peter, 1944–
    Firetrucks/Peter Brady
    p. cm.
    Includes bibliographical references and index.
    Summary: An introduction to firetrucks, what they carry, and what they do.
    ISBN 1-56065-350-7
    1. Fire engines--Juvenile literature. [1. Fire engines.] I. Title.
TH9372.B73 1996
628.9'25--dc20

                                95-47780
                                CIP
                                 AC

Photo credits
Unicorn/Eric R. Berndt: 10
Unicorn/Deneve Feigh Bunde: 12, 14
Peter Ford: 4, 6, 8, 16
Unicorn/Dede Gilman: 20
Unicorn/Joe Sohm: 18
Unicorn/Aneal Vohra: cover

Table of Contents

Words in **boldface** type in the text are defined in the Words to Know section in the back of this book.

Firetrucks

Firetrucks carry firefighters and their tools to fires. Different trucks are used for different kinds of fires.

The Fire Engine

The fire engine is an all-purpose truck. It carries ladders and hoses. It can pump water from its own tank. It can pump water from a **hydrant**, too.

Ladder Trucks

Some firetrucks have long ladders on **turntables**. Some have platforms or cages at the end of the ladder. These are used to carry firefighters high up on buildings.

Elevated Platform Trucks

Elevated platform trucks have a **boom** but no ladder. Either a cage or a nozzle is at the end of the boom. The boom is used to get water and people to high places.

Pumper Trucks

Pumper trucks carry their own supply of water in a tank. They can also pump water from a stream or pond. They are used for fires in the country, where there are no hydrants.

Foam Trucks

Foam trucks are used at airports. They pump foam to put out burning airplane fuel. Water will not put out burning airplane fuel.

Chemical Firetrucks

Many chemical and electrical fires cannot be put out with water. Oil companies and other industries have special trucks for these fires. They use liquid chemicals and powders to put out fires.

Fireboats

Fireboats put out fires in **harbors** or on **piers**. A fireboat pumps water from the harbor onto the fire.

Helicopters and Airplanes

When a fire is in the forest, helicopters and airplanes do the job of a firetruck. They spray or drop chemicals to smother the flames. Firefighters on the ground help by spraying water on the land.

Hands On: Be a Smoke Detector Ranger

1. Make sure there are smoke detectors outside each sleeping area where you live.
2. Make sure there is a smoke detector on each level of your home, including the basement.
3. Test your smoke detectors once a month.
4. Change the batteries in your smoke detectors once a year.

Fire Safety Tips

• Never play with matches.
• Know two different ways to get out of the place where you live.
• Practice fire drills with your family.
• If there is a fire, get out and leave your things behind.
• If you see or smell smoke, crawl low and get out.
• If your clothes catch on fire, stop, drop, and roll.

Words to Know

boom—long metal tube that folds out to reach high places

harbor—area where ships anchor

hydrant—pipe on street corner from which firefighters get water

pier—long, narrow platform built over water, usually made of wood

turntable—round platform that can turn all the way around

Read More

Bingham, Caroline. *Fire Truck.* New York: Dorling Kindersley, 1995.

Gibbons, Gail. *Fire! Fire!* New York: Thomas Y. Crowell, 1984.

Kuklin, Susan. *Fighting Fires.* New York: Bradbury Press, 1993.

Maass, Rob. *Fire Fighters.* New York: Scholastic, 1989.

Index

1/14. 8/04 2-8-05